The Great Ice Battle

A Magical World Awaits You
Read

#1 The Hidden Stairs and the Magic Carpet

#2 Journey to the Volcano Palace

#3 The Mysterious Island

#4 City in the Clouds

#5 The Great Ice Battle

**The Great
Ice Battle**

by Tony Abbott
Illustrated by Tim Jessell

SCHOLASTIC INC.
New York Toronto London Auckland Sydney
Mexico City New Delhi Hong Kong Buenos Aires

To Dolores,
without whom none
of this would be

Book design by Dawn Adelman

ISBN-13: 978-0-590-10843-0
ISBN-10: 0-590-10843-3

32 31 30 29 28 27 26 25   10 11 12/0

Printed in the U.S.A.   40
First Scholastic printing, December 1999

Contents

1. Daymare!   1

2. City of Light   12

3. White Snow, Dark Magic   21

4. A Party of Evil Dudes   30

5. The Gift of Magic   38

6. The Red Wolves of Droon   47

7. A Royal Wizard   55

8. Race Against Time   63

9. Droonians, Unite!   70

10. Reverse the Curse!   78

One

Daymare!

As cold as ice.

That's how Eric Hinkle felt as he jumped from his bed.

"Brrr!" he said to himself, shivering. He pulled on his thick socks. He got into his warmest winter pants. He shivered again. Eric was having bad thoughts of an evil sorcerer. And that's what was giving him the creeps — but not why he was so cold.

Ever since Eric and his best friends, Julie and Neal, had discovered the entrance to the amazing, secret world of Droon, they had been afraid of Lord Sparr.

"Who wouldn't be afraid?" Eric said aloud.

With those creepy purple fins growing up behind his ears. And the long black cloak. And his ugly red-faced warriors called Ninns.

Sparr was the reason Eric felt so cold.

The evil sorcerer wanted only one thing.

To take over all of Droon.

"But now, things in Droon are different," Eric said as he dug in his closet for his winter coat.

On their last adventure in Droon, Sparr had had a chance to hurt Eric. But he hadn't done it.

He had let him live. He'd said Eric would *help* him.

"I'll never help you!" Eric said with a shudder.

"Why won't you help me?"

"Because you're evil!" Eric snapped back.

"Eric!"

He blinked. His father was standing in the doorway to his room. He was frowning.

"Dad!" Eric said. "I'm sorry. You're not evil. I guess I was daydreaming or something."

His father sighed. "Well, you can help me later. Neal and Julie are waiting for you outside."

"Thanks!" Eric threw on his coat and ran downstairs to the back door. Still shivering, he grabbed his cap, pulled it low over his eyes, and wrapped his scarf tight around his neck.

He flung open the door. "Whoa!" he gasped.

Warm air and bright sunshine poured in.

Julie and Neal were dressed in T-shirts and shorts. They had a softball, mitts, and a bat.

"It's not hockey season!" Neal said, chuckling.

Julie made a face. "Are you okay, Eric?"

He stared at his friends. Then he tore off his coat and scarf. "This is sooooo weird! I was cold. I was freezing! I must have daydreamed that it was winter! Sorry."

Julie tossed the ball up. "So, who's pitching?"

"Me first!" Neal grabbed the ball from Julie.

"No, me!" said Eric.

"Sorry, pal. I called it," said Neal. "Besides, I've got this new throw to show you! I just twist my fingers and shoot the ball. It's fast!"

Eric took the bat, but in his mind he kept seeing Lord Sparr.

"Why don't we use *ice* today?" Sparr was saying.

Ice. That was the other thing Sparr had said the last time they were in Droon. Sparr was going to do something bad with ice.

"We'll defeat Princess Keeah," the Sparr in Eric's mind continued. "And the old wizard, Galen. You will help me. . . ."

"No way!" Eric cried, dropping the bat. "I'll never do it! Never!"

"Are you going to play or not?" Neal said.

Eric turned to his friends. "Sorry, guys. But something weird is going on. I keep

seeing Sparr in my mind. He's telling me how I'm going to help him. It's like a nightmare, only it's daytime."

"A daymare!" Julie said. Then she gasped. "Wait a second. Do you think the daydreams mean we need to go to Droon?"

Their friend Princess Keeah had told them that when they dreamed about Droon, it meant the magic was working.

It meant they needed to return.

Eric nodded slowly. "This might be some kind of message or something." He started for the back steps. "We need to re-turn. Now."

"What? No!" Neal jumped up and down. "I need to show you my new twisty throw — hey!"

But Julie and Eric were already in the house.

"Oh, man!" said Neal. "I knew we weren't going to play this game. I just knew it!"

By the time Neal caught up with them, Eric and Julie were halfway down the basement stairs.

"We'll play when we get back," Julie said. "It's not as if Droon takes any time. No matter how long our adventure is, we come back around the same time we left. It's so neat that way."

This was true. One of the very coolest things the kids discovered was that it took no time at all to have a full adventure in Droon.

"Time is strange there," Eric said. "It's different from here in the Upper World."

The Upper World was Droon's name for where the kids lived.

Neal set the softball on the workbench. Julie and Eric pushed aside a large box.

Behind it was the door to a small empty room under the basement stairs.

Carefully, they went inside the room. Eric closed the door behind them. Julie clicked off the light.

For an instant the room was dark, then —

Whoosh! A set of rainbow-colored stairs appeared where the floor used to be.

"I love that!" Julie whispered.

Eric took the first step. "Let's go."

They began their descent.

"I can't see anything but the stairs," Eric whispered. "It's totally dark all around."

Julie took a deep breath. "Do you think the stairs can lead us to someplace bad?"

"Thanks for scaring me," Neal mumbled, clutching the stair rail.

"I'm not sure," said Eric. "I guess that's one of Droon's many secrets — whoa!"

"What is it?" asked Neal, huddling closer.

"That was the bottom step," said Eric.

No sooner had they stepped off than the stairway began to fade. A moment later, it was gone.

"No turning back now," said Julie.

They stepped forward. Eric stuck his hands out. "I think it's some kind of cave. The walls are rough. So is the floor. Be careful."

"It smells like animals," Julie added.

Grrrr!

Everyone stopped.

"Is somebody going to say 'Excuse me,' or are we in deep trouble?" Neal asked.

Grrrr! The growling noise was closer this time.

"I hear breathing," Julie whispered.

"And I s-s-see . . . eyes!" Neal stammered. "Red eyes! Lots of them!"

Eric shivered again, then whispered, "Everyone who agrees we should run, say 'Run.'"

"RUN!" they all cried.

They ran.

Two

City of Light

The three friends scrambled through the cave as fast as they could.

Grrr! Grrr! Whatever was behind them was following swiftly.

"There's light up ahead!" Julie called back.

"I'm there!" said Neal.

"Last one out is a rotten egg!" Eric cried.

They hurled themselves out of the mouth of the cave and into the light. Bright light. And green grass. And flowers. They tripped over a low wall and tumbled down a short slope to a wire fence.

"We're trapped!" Neal yelled.

Suddenly, the kids heard laughter.

They sat up and squinted through the fence.

Standing behind it were Princess Keeah and her father, King Zello.

"Welcome to Droon!" the king boomed.

They looked back at the cave. The red eyes blinked and disappeared into the darkness.

Eric jumped to his feet. "You mean . . . we're safe?"

"Very," Keeah said with a giggle. "You just looked funny running out of the wolves' cave."

Neal gulped. "Did you say . . . *wolves?* Man, I hope we never go back into that cave!"

Keeah and her father opened an iron gate and helped the three kids outside the fence.

"The red wolves of Droon are famous," King Zello said. "They protect our city!"

The king was a tall man with broad shoulders. He wore a helmet with horns and carried a wooden club. Princess Keeah had long blonde hair. She wore a green tunic and leather boots.

"Welcome to Jaffa City," Keeah said. "Jaffa is the royal city of Droon!"

The princess led them out to a stone courtyard that was larger than a baseball stadium.

At one side was a busy marketplace. Men and women strolled and shopped at colorful tents. Their children played happily by a beautiful fountain nearby.

"Wow," said Eric. "I had bad daydreams

about Sparr. But things look pretty okay here!"

On the other side of the square rose giant buildings of white and silver and green and pink stone. In between grew flowers and bushes, and birds sang in white-blossomed apple trees.

A soft breeze blew across the vast open space.

"It sure is beautiful," Julie said as they passed the fountain. The children of Droon waved to the three friends from the Upper World.

"Friendly, too," Neal said, giving the kids the peace sign.

"And someday Keeah will rule over this city as well as all the villages outside," the king said. "Just like her mother, Queen Relna."

Keeah's mother was a wizard who had

been transformed into a white falcon. In that shape, she had helped the kids fight Lord Sparr. Now she herself needed help to become human again.

"But for now, Keeah," the king said, "you must get ready for your magic lessons. Galen will be here soon. Max will come, too, of course."

Galen was a powerful old wizard. Max was his spider-troll assistant.

The king beamed with pride and said, "Galen tells me that in some ways Keeah's powers are greater than his own. When the time is right, her true powers will be revealed."

Eric's eyes went wide. "Powers? Cool!"

Keeah made a face. "More like lukewarm. So far, I've broken seven clay pots, one bowl, a chair, and two clocks."

"Three clocks," her father said, smiling.

"But Galen will teach you. And look, here he comes!"

A thick blue mist rose in the middle of the square. Sparks of light streaked through it.

An instant later — *zamm*! A bearded old man in a long blue robe stood there. Next to him sat a large spider with four arms and four legs. He had a round face, a pug nose, and orange hair that stood straight up.

"Galen! Max!" Eric said. "Good to see you again!"

But the wizard did not look happy.

"What's wrong?" the king asked, gripping his wooden club tightly.

There was fear in Max's eyes as he spoke. "Terrible!" he chittered. "Lord Sparr! He's coming!"

"I fear the worst," Galen said. "A curse

has been sent by the evil one. We've tracked it across the plains. Now look!"

Galen pointed to the skies above them. A vast black cloud passed quickly in front of the sun. The entire courtyard fell into shadow.

"It is a curse!" Max muttered.

Eric thought of his daydream again. He shivered with cold as he shot a look at Keeah.

"What kind of curse?" he asked.

A snowflake fell from the darkening sky. Another followed it. Then another and another.

The sun vanished completely. The air grew icy cold. Freezing wind tore across the city.

The trees that had been so beautiful were instantly crusted with heavy frost.

Ice formed on the city walls and on the stones of the courtyard.

Eric remembered what Sparr had said. "Ice!" he cried, shivering. "Sparr is using ice to attack us! It's just like he told me!"

Keeah's eyes went wide with fear. "Oh, my Jaffa City!"

Three

White Snow, Dark Magic

Within moments the city was covered with ice. Biting winds swirled snow into huge drifts.

"This is Sparr's dark magic!" Galen said.

Crrrack! The fountain's silvery stream thickened and suddenly went still.

"This is just like my daydream," Eric said. "It's a curse of ice."

The colorful banners over the marketplace stopped waving. Icicles formed on the buildings and hung like daggers over the frozen streets.

Eric saw the fear in Keeah's eyes. He shivered, too. "What can we do to stop this?"

Keeah turned to the king. "Our villages can't survive this cold. We must save our people!"

Zello nodded. "I shall go help the villagers. Keeah, you stay here and keep Jaffa City safe. Galen, I must go quickly. Perhaps your latest invention . . ."

"Ah!" the wizard said. "My water sled. Yes, it should ride quite well on ice. Follow me!" Galen led the king and his guards to the stables.

"We'll help, too!" Neal said, clapping his arms around himself. "If we don't fr-fr-freeze f-first!"

Max scuttled over. "Let me make you

warm!" he chirped. "I'll spin you coats of my special spider silk. It's the warmest fabric in all of Droon!"

Max's arms and legs began to blur in the air all around the kids. Soon, he had woven each one a thick coat and a pair of furry boots.

"Thank you," said Julie. "They're very warm."

A moment later, several shaggy six-legged beasts called pilkas trotted across the square to the gate.

In the lead was Leep, Galen's own pet pilka.

Behind them, the pilkas dragged a sleek wooden sled. It looked like a small boat and rode over the ice on long skis. King Zello, bundled in a cloak of bright blue fur, was riding in the back.

"Be careful!" Keeah said, hugging her father.

"I shall be. And you, too," he replied.

Errrr! Two guards pushed aside a large bolt and the city's huge iron gates swung open.

The king snapped the reins, and Leep charged ahead, pulling Galen's sled into the swirling snow.

Keeah waved one last time before — *clong!* — the gates closed.

"I predict he will be safe," Galen said.

Neal frowned. "But, um, what about us? Could Sparr just march in here with his Ninns?"

Keeah beamed. "Galen charmed our walls! An evil spirit can't enter unless he is invited."

"That is true," the wizard said. "An old spell."

"And we never *will* invite evil ones into Jaffa!" Max chittered. "They have no manners!"

"Excellent," said Neal. "I like being safe for a change."

Keeah smiled. "Now, everyone, come. Let's get warm in the throne room!"

Julie and Neal hurried in after Keeah. The guards went with Galen into the frosted palace. Max scuttled across the stones after his master.

But Eric stayed behind for a moment. He climbed to the top of the wall and looked out. The nearby villages were quickly being swallowed up by the deep snow.

He shuddered. But it wasn't from the cold.

Did I make this happen somehow? he wondered. *Did I already help Sparr do this? How?*

"No! I couldn't have done this!" he shouted into the storm. "And I won't help Sparr, either! Never! Ever!"

He turned to go into the palace.

"Help!" a tiny voice cried out.

Eric looked down. The courtyard below was empty of everything but ice and snow.

"Help!" the voice called out again.

Eric looked back over the wall. There, in the deepening snow, was a small figure. A boy.

The boy shivered in thin clothes, his tiny arms wrapped around him. He looked just like the children playing in the square before.

"Help me!" the boy pleaded. "I was playing. I got left outside."

Eric turned to the gates. "Guards!" he yelled.

But the guards had gone inside with Galen.

The only sound was the red wolves starting to howl from their cave.

The little boy trembled even more.

"Wait a second! Hold on!" Eric yelled. He ran down the steps to the front gate.

He could hear the child whimpering outside. "Wait!" Eric called. With all his strength he pushed the gate's huge bolt aside. Then he dug his feet into the snow and pulled on the giant door. It wouldn't budge. He pulled harder.

Finally, it opened a tiny crack.

Eric peered into the swirling winds. Ice pelted his face. "Where are you?" he shouted.

The wolves howled again.

So did the wind.

"Cold!" the boy said. He stood a few feet from the iron door, the storm whipping at his ragged clothes. He was nearly covered in ice.

"So cold!" the boy groaned.

"Come in!" Eric cried, reaching for the boy. "Get warm inside!"

The boy leaped past Eric. He was through the gates in a single bound.

"Thank you," the boy said. Then he turned and looked Eric straight in the eye. He grinned.

"I told you that you would help me!" he said.

Eric gasped. "What do you mean? Wait . . . no . . . no!"

The wolves howled a final time.

And the boy's face began to change.

Four

A Party of Evil Dudes

The small boy's pale skin turned the color of ashes. Then he wiggled and stretched himself up to the size of a tall man.

"No . . . no . . ." Eric mumbled. "It can't be!"

The figure's narrow shoulders broadened. His rags fell away to reveal a long black cloak. But the worst part was the purple fins that sprouted behind his ears.

"Sparr is here!" Eric cried. "Help!"

He raced as fast as he could to the palace.

Galen ran down the steps. A dozen armed guards dashed out with him. "Eric, what is it?"

"I messed up! I messed up big-time!" Eric said, falling to the steps, his heart racing with fear. "Sparr tricked me! I let him in! I helped him!"

Neal, Julie, and Keeah rushed to Eric.

"Hide, all of you," the wizard said sharply, striding out to the courtyard. "Guards, come!"

The four kids crept out as far as they could, then ducked behind a tall snowdrift. Max skittered out of the palace and huddled with them.

"How stupid could I be?" Eric groaned softly.

Lord Sparr stood by the gate. His deep

eyes flickered and blazed red. His transformation was complete.

"Seize him!" Galen called out. A dozen of the king's soldiers quickly surrounded Sparr.

The sorcerer bared his teeth in an evil grin. "How rude to treat an invited guest with such . . . coldness!" His fingers sparked suddenly.

"Galen, watch out!" Keeah cried. She raised her own hand. A beam of pale light shot from it.

It fizzled and vanished in an instant.

Blam! Sparr's bolt struck the wizard. Galen was thrown backward in the snow.

Then he stopped moving.

His blue robe went stiff. His long white hair and beard turned to ice. Frost crept over his cheeks, his forehead, his nose.

"Oh, Galen!" Max whimpered. "No . . . no . . ."

The wizard's eyes went glassy. "So cold!" he said. Then he said no more.

Before the guards could move — *kkkk!* Another bolt of light shot from Sparr. The guards turned to ice as quickly as Galen had.

The wolves howled deep in their cave. Sparr smiled. "Yes, even you shall fall to my curse."

Kkkk! Blam! The wolves howled no more.

"We've got to stop this guy!" Eric whispered.

Boom-boom-boom! There came a loud knocking on the gates. Sparr turned. With a flick of his wrist, the gates opened. "Come, my Ninns!"

"Oh, great!" Neal groaned. "Now he's inviting his Ninns in, too! A regular party of evil dudes!"

Twenty of Sparr's heavy-footed, red-faced Ninn warriors clomped into the courtyard.

Some of them carried huge hammers over their shoulders. Others had bows and arrows.

They grunted and bowed before their master.

"You four, bring me the amulet of Zor," the sorcerer commanded.

"Yes, Lord Sparr," growled the chief Ninn.

"You three, take the old wizard to the throne room," Sparr said. "The rest of you, find the children. The boy helped me get in. But his usefulness is done. Now, destroy them all!"

Sparr swirled his cloak and swept up the steps into the palace.

The children quaked with fear.

"Keeah," whispered Julie. "You must know a spell against this. Don't you have some magic that will unfreeze the wizard?"

Keeah hung her head. "My magic failed when I needed it most." Her tears fell to the ground and turned to ice.

"Don't despair, princess," Max whispered. "Galen will be fine. At least . . . I hope he will!"

"Well, there's got to be something we can do," said Eric.

Neal turned to Eric. "A . . ."

"A what?" Eric asked. "You have an idea?"

"A . . . a . . ." Neal said, shivering.

"Tell us!" Julie whispered.

"A . . . a . . . *choo!*" Neal sneezed loudly.

"Huh?" grunted one of the Ninns in the courtyard. He pointed to the drift where the kids were hiding. "Snow . . . sneeze?"

"Not snow! Little ones!" shouted another.

The Ninns loaded their bows and arrows.

"That's our cue to get out of here!" Julie said.

"Let's hide in the market," Keeah said. "We can lose the Ninns there!"

"Better than losing our lives *here*!" Neal said.

The five friends bolted up in a swirl of snow and took off across the courtyard.

The angry Ninns clomped right after them!

Five

The Gift of Magic

Thwang! Thwang!

Arrows whizzed past the kids as they dashed across the snowy courtyard. The arrows plinked and clanked against the frosted stones.

"Head for the rows of market stalls!" Keeah said, pointing ahead. "We can hide there!"

Max skittered on the stones behind

Keeah. "Oh, if only my master, Galen, were here!"

They darted into the thick of the marketplace. The tents were crusted with snow and ice. Men and women stood by their tables. But they weren't moving. They were completely frozen.

"This is so sad," said Julie, out of breath.

"I know them," Keeah added.

Clomp! Crash! The Ninns burst through the first row of stalls searching for the kids. They tore down the tents and overturned the tables.

"Oh, dear!" Max chittered. "Terrible brutes!"

"I agree!" said Eric, hurrying past a stall filled with barrels of sugar and flour.

Clomp! Ninns were storming around from behind. Soon they would see the kids.

"Ninn sandwich!" Neal said. "We're trapped!"

"I've got an idea!" Eric whispered. Then he grabbed Neal and pushed his face into one of the sugar barrels.

"Hey!" Neal yelped, pulling himself back up, his face covered with white sugar. "What are you doing? I mean — mmm. That's good sugar."

"Shhh!" Eric gasped. "Pretend you're frozen!"

"Huh?" Then Neal's eyes went wide. "Oh, I get it! The sugar looks like frost!" He went stiff.

Julie and Keeah got the idea, too. They stuck their faces in the sugar barrel, then popped back up. They stood as still as statues.

Eric did the same. So did Max.

Their faces were completely frosted in sugar.

They held their breaths.

Clomp! Clank! Two red Ninns in black armor stomped between the stalls to the children.

"Child?" growled one. He poked one of his six claws at Neal's nose. He waved the other in front of Eric's face. Both boys stared straight ahead. They didn't move. They didn't breathe.

"Frozen?" the Ninn said.

The other Ninn peered at Keeah. Then he pushed his big red face down close to Julie's. His dark, beady eyes stared into hers.

"Frozen," he grunted to his fellow Ninn.

They wandered away noisily between the stalls. Finally they headed back to the palace.

Eric let out a long breath. "That was close!"

"Real close," Neal said, brushing the sugar from his cheeks. "I never knew food could save your life!"

"Let's get out of here," said Julie. "Before that big lug decides to breathe on me again —"

"Shhh!" Keeah said. "I hear something."

The kids stood still and listened.

Eric looked up. "It sounds like . . . wings!"

"It's Queen Relna!" Max exclaimed. "Look!"

Down through the swirling snow came a white falcon. She fluttered slowly above them.

"Mother!" the princess said softly.

"Keeah, my child," the falcon said. "How I can speak to you, I do not know. But Keeah . . . only you have the power to save our city."

"My magic failed!" Keeah replied. "I

couldn't help Galen. I tried to, but Sparr froze him!"

"And it's all my fault," Eric muttered.

The bird spoke again. "Sometimes bad things happen for a reason. We need to be tested, so that we grow stronger. Keeah, remember who you are. And know this: True magic comes from a magic heart."

Then the bird hovered over the barrel of sugar. From her eyes came a spiral of blue light.

The light fell on the sugar. The sugar began to sparkle.

"Hurry!" said the queen. "You have but a little time left before what is frozen remains frozen!"

Then, with a rapid flutter of wings, Keeah's mother was gone.

"Wow, is that magic dust?" Julie asked.

Eric remembered how Keeah had once

sprinkled shiny powder on his sprained an-
kle, curing him.

The princess tossed a handful of the
sparkling crystals in the air and watched
them fall. "I think it is magic," she said.

"Then let's get to the palace right away
and try the dust on Galen," Eric said.

"Excuse me," Neal said, raising his
hand. "But Sparr is in there, with a million
nasty Ninns."

"Neal's right," Keeah said. She filled a
velvet pouch on her belt with the powder.
"We'll need some help first."

"Good thinking!" Neal said. He dipped
his finger in the barrel of sugar and licked
it. "Mmm. It's magic, but it still tastes
good."

Eric turned to Keeah. "Should we wait
here for your father to get back with an
army of big, tough Droon guys?"

Keeah shook her head. "We can't wait. We need other friends to help us. Old friends."

Neal gulped. "Hold on a second. You're not talking about those wolves, are you?"

Keeah patted her velvet pouch. "We need to unfreeze them."

"You *are* talking about those wolves!" Neal yelped. "Oh, man! I knew we were going back to that cave! I just knew it!"

The princess had already grabbed Julie and Eric and started to run.

"To the cave, everyone!" she cried. "Hurry!"

Six

The Red Wolves of Droon

"It's like a tomb in here," Eric said as they entered the cave. "And darker than I remember it."

"Thanks for scaring me again," said Neal.

Keeah pulled a flaming torch from the wall outside and handed it to Max. She took another for herself. "It gets even darker down below."

Carefully, the five friends tiptoed into

the darkness. Soon, the rocky cave floor gave way to rough, carved steps.

Sssss! The torches sizzled as the thick ice on the ceiling melted down onto the flames.

Eric felt bad about letting Sparr in. There was nothing he could do now, except help make it right. He hoped they could reverse the curse.

"How did the wolves get here?" he asked.

Keeah stepped carefully down the frosted steps. "Long ago, a terrible creature named Zor fought the wolves who lived in the hills here."

"Who is Zor?" asked Julie.

Keeah took a deep breath. "He was a giant."

"A terrible giant! If the stories are to be believed," Max said with a shiver.

"My mother took the giant's power

away," Keeah said. "He vanished. Finally, he died."

Max nodded. "To thank Relna, the wolves promised to guard forever the amulet that gave Zor his power."

"What's an amulet?" Neal asked.

"A kind of crest," Keeah said. "A big piece of jewelry with a crystal in the center. It's hidden below our city, in the cavern of the wolves."

"So that's what Sparr is after!" Eric said.

Julie frowned. "But if Zor is dead, what exactly will Sparr do with the giant's old jewelry?"

"I don't know," Keeah whispered. "But something tells me we'll find out soon enough."

They stepped off the final step onto a smooth floor. Before them was an opening into a stone room. Beyond that was an even smaller room.

"Oh, no!" Julie gasped. "The poor wolves!"

There, in the flickering torchlight, were three large wolves.

One lay motionless near the entrance to the inner room. Another was standing on all fours, its long ears pointed up, its eyes as still as glass. A third crouched by the stairs, its fangs bared, as if ready to pounce. The bright red fur of each wolf was now silvery-white with ice.

All three were frozen solid.

"Just like my master," Max chirped softly.

"According to the old stories, there was only one thing that could stop them," Keeah said.

"Let me guess. Being frozen," Eric said. "And that's why Sparr used a curse of ice to attack the city. He knew he could get Zor's amulet."

"He already did," Julie said. She pointed to the inner room. It was empty.

Neal joined her and gazed up. "There's a hole in the ceiling here. The Ninns must have busted their way in with those nasty hammers."

Max shot sticky silk at the ceiling and swung up to the hole. "I'll see what I can find out."

Keeah took a deep breath and opened her velvet bag. She sprinkled powder on the wolves.

Zzzz! The air sizzled over the frozen beasts.

"It's working!" Eric said. "The magic is working!"

The creatures' eyes softened instantly.

One wolf yawned and stretched. The others shook themselves from head to tail, spraying a thousand icy needles across the stones.

"Yes!" Julie cried. "They're alive!"

Keeah knelt and whispered to the red wolves. *"Sama teku mey?"* The animals seemed to answer her with purring sounds and soft growling.

She has the power, Eric thought. He glanced at his friends. Their eyes were wide with wonder.

Keeah turned back to the kids. "I must help Galen. Even if it means facing Sparr. I must trust the magic. That's what my mother's words mean."

"Her words mean something to us, too," Eric agreed.

Max swung back into the room. "Those nasty Ninns are taking Zor's amulet to the throne room. Sparr is waiting for it there."

Keeah's eyes flashed. "The king's room? Only my father should sit there!"

The wolves growled, sensing Keeah's anger.

"We'll bring your father back," said Eric. "We'll make things right again. We have to."

Julie nodded. "We'll do it."

"We make a great team," Neal added.

Keeah smiled. "Then come. We have work to do!"

Seven

A Royal Wizard

They climbed up a secret passage and came out a small door on the main level of the palace.

Max peered around in all directions. "No Ninns," he chirped. "As long as we're quiet!"

"The throne room is not far from here," Keeah said. "Everybody, follow me."

Eric crept close to the frosty walls. Julie

and Neal were right behind him. The red wolves padded silently next to Keeah.

Soon they were outside the throne room.

Eric and Neal peered around one side of the doorway, Julie and Keeah around the other.

The throne room was large and round. The walls were covered with tapestries. The floor was tiled in a strange pattern of colored stones.

Eric had seen that pattern before, in Galen's secret tower. The throne room's floor was a giant map of Droon.

Sparr sat in the king's large golden throne.

Galen stood nearby, as white and unmoving as a statue carved of stone.

"Bring the amulet to me!" Sparr commanded.

Grrr! The wolves growled behind Keeah.

"Hush!" she said, patting their heads. "Soon."

Four big Ninn soldiers carried an iron box into the room. They set it down in front of their master, opened the box, and bowed.

With both hands Sparr reached in and pulled out a large black object. He held it over his head.

It was a long triangle piercing a circle. Horns stuck out from either side.

A glittering crystal hung in the center of the triangle.

"Behold the amulet of Zor!" Sparr cried out.

The Ninns bowed before the strange object.

The amulet sparkled in the torchlight.

"Soon, we shall begin our long journey," Sparr announced. "Zor . . . we shall come to you!"

"Oh, dear!" Max whispered.

Then Lord Sparr drew his sword. He attached the amulet to the handle and tightened it.

"What is he doing?" Julie asked.

Keeah frowned. "I don't know."

The sorcerer strode to the center of the room.

He stood over the spot where the colored tiles showed the outline of Jaffa City. "Soon our questions will be answered," he said.

He clutched his sword with both hands.

He pointed the blade down.

With one powerful thrust — *clong!* — Sparr sank his blade deep into the floor.

Deep into the map of Jaffa City.

"What is going on —" Eric began.

Suddenly, the amulet's crystal lit up. It began glowing bright green. It sparked and hissed.

Keeah stood up. "It's time," she said.

"We'll bring back the king," Eric said firmly.

The princess took a deep breath. "Good luck."

"To you, too," said Julie, smiling at her.

Keeah stepped from the shadows. *"Detchu-tah!"* she called out sharply.

In a flash, the three large red wolves roared into the throne room. They growled and bared their fangs. Steam rose from their open jaws as they skittered by Keeah's side.

Sparr stepped back. Fear crossed his face. "The wolves? They were frozen! So . . . you *are* your mother's daughter. Too bad your little show of magic won't last very long."

"Long enough to stop you!" Keeah said. She raised her hands at Sparr.

Eric felt his blood go cold, then hot. "Maybe we should stay to help her. This is all my fault."

"Sometimes bad things happen for a reason," Max said. "Perhaps Keeah was meant to do this. I shall stay here. Galen would want me to. But you, you must find the king."

"But —" Eric started.

Julie grabbed Eric's arm. "Keeah has powers. She's got to fight Sparr. And we've got to do this!"

Neal grabbed Eric's other arm. "Let's go!"

As the wolves leaped for Sparr and his

Ninns, the three friends scrambled through the halls.

They shivered as they dashed down the steps.

Their hearts raced as they entered a world of ice.

Eight

Race Against Time

Julie and Eric hitched up reins and saddles on three shaggy pilkas while Neal wrestled open the large city gate.

"Let's find the king!" Eric said firmly, snapping the reins of his pilka.

"Giddyap!" Neal shouted, jumping on his own.

At once, the pilkas took off. They raced past the city gates and out over the crunchy ground. The storm wrapped around them swiftly.

Soon, the palace was out of sight.

"King Zello!" Eric cried.

His voice was lost in the howling wind.

"The storm is getting worse!" said Julie.

"And it's nearly nighttime!" Neal shouted. "Perfect time for this kind of nightmare!"

Still, the six-legged pilkas galloped on. They stormed through an icy forest. Icicles fell like daggers from frozen branches. Tall trees cracked in half, their black limbs heavy with silver ice.

"This place really is cursed," said Julie.

Neal cupped his hands together. "King Zello!" he yelled. "Oh, man, he'll never hear us. He could be miles away. He could even be —"

"Don't say it!" Eric cried, standing in his

saddle. He called out even louder. "Zello! Zello!"

The wind roared like Sparr's deep laughter.

Eric's arms and legs ached. He felt cold. He felt like going to sleep. Frost began to form on all their cheeks. It was getting darker. And colder.

"No!" Eric cried, snapping the reins again. "We have to do this! We have to make it right! Keep yelling, everybody! Keep yelling!"

"King Zello!" they shouted at the top of their lungs. "King Zello!"

Then, they heard it. A faraway sound.

A familiar noise above the wild snowstorm.

Hrrr!

"Hey! I'd recognize that sound anywhere!" Julie shouted. "It's Leep!"

"Yes!" Eric cried. "And where Leep is, there's — King Zello! Zello!"

A dark shape galloped suddenly toward them.

It was Leep. And on the sled behind him, King Zello.

The king pulled up sharply on the reins.

"Galen is frozen!" Eric cried, jumping from his pilka. "And Sparr and Keeah are fighting! There are lots of Ninns, too. A whole army of Ninns!"

"I have an army, too," the king said. He waved his hand behind him.

"Whoa!" Eric exclaimed.

Behind the king, riding on their own sleds, were dozens of men and women. But mostly there were children. Lots and lots of children.

"Wow, an army of Droon kids!" Neal said.

"But how will we fight the big Ninns?" one young girl asked.

Julie jumped down from her saddle. "Hey, I just thought of something. With this curse, we almost forgot the best thing about snow."

Neal frowned. "What's that?"

Julie dug her hands into a high drift and grinned. "The good old Upper World . . . snowball!"

The children of Droon crowded around them.

"We'll help, too," one of them said. "We want to keep our city free."

"And maybe we can use these!" one boy said. From his coat he pulled a Y-shaped stick.

"A slingshot?" said Ned. "Cool! But you have to remember rule number one. When you're fighting Ninns, you pack your snowballs hard!"

The children of Droon dug into the snow eagerly. Soon everyone had made dozens of snowballs. They filled their pockets with them.

"To the palace!" the king called out. At once his sled thundered across the snow.

"Yahoo!" Eric said as he snapped the reins of his pilka. "Sparr and his Ninns will never know what hit them!"

Nine

Droonians, Unite!

The armored red warriors were waiting on the palace steps as the sleds and pilkas roared into the city.

"Come on, everybody!" Eric said, gathering the kids of Droon together. "Snowballs out!"

"Snowballs out!" the kids replied.

"Ready," said Neal. "Aim —"

"And . . . fire!" shouted Julie.

Splat! Splat! Splat!

"Aggkh!" the Ninns cried. Half of them dropped their bows. The other half fell to the steps, clutching their shoulders and knees.

"Yes!" Neal whooped. "Kids one, Ninns zero!"

"To the throne room!" King Zello shouted, rushing past the Ninns and into the palace.

Blam! Crash! Kkkk! Poom!

When they entered the round room, Keeah and Sparr were flinging lightning bolts at each other.

"Whoa!" said Eric. "Keeah is awesome! I guess she figured out the magic!"

A band of angry Ninns rushed at the kids, but the red wolves lunged, forcing the Ninns back.

Then Max swung down from the ceiling and sprayed sticky silk on them.

"Excellent!" Julie shouted. "Come on,

kids, let's finish the job!" She and the children of Droon pelted the tangled Ninns with snowballs.

King Zello led the grown-ups in a charge at Sparr. "Keeah, help Galen!" he boomed.

Keeah rushed to the old wizard, reaching for her velvet pouch.

Fwing! A Ninn arrow whizzed by her side. Keeah looked down. The pouch was slit in half.

The sparkling dust spilled across the floor!

"Oh, no —" she cried.

Blam! Sparr hurled a bolt at Keeah, knocking her roughly into her father. They fell to the floor.

Eric looked around. "I'm going for the amulet!" he cried. "Neal, cover me!"

"You got it!" Neal yelled. "Finally, I get

to try my twisty fastball!" He pelted Sparr with snowballs all the way.

Splat! Splat! Splat! The sorcerer fell back.

Eric took a long slide toward the amulet. Suddenly — *kkkk-blam!*

A beam of green light shot out from the amulet's crystal. Its light blasted the stone floor.

"Umph!" Eric was thrown backward into Neal. They hit the floor hard. Near them, the giant map of Droon glowed where the beam hit.

Sparr began to laugh wildly. "Yes! Yes! Yes!"

"What, what, what?" Neal snapped.

"The Dust Hills of Panjibarrh!" the sorcerer howled. "That is where great Zor lies sleeping!"

"Sleeping?" said Eric. "But isn't he dead?"

"The giant shall rise again!" Sparr cried. His fins turned black. He pulled his sword out of the floor. Then he towered over Eric and Neal.

"Um . . . any ideas, pal?" Eric mumbled.

Neal shrugged. He dug his hands into his pockets. "Sorry, man. Out of ammo."

"I'm not!" Keeah cried. In a single motion, she twirled to her feet, faced Sparr, and thrust out both of her hands. Before he could move —

KKKK-BLAM! The room went totally white.

"Ahhhhh!" Eric screamed, shutting his eyes.

"Yeeooww!" Neal yelped, covering his face.

But when the light vanished, Sparr was slumped against the wall.

"You!" he shrieked at the princess. "You

have wounded me!" He fell to the floor, yowling in pain like an injured animal.

He clutched the amulet tightly. "All of you will pay for this!"

Ninns surrounded him and pulled him to his feet. Waving their weapons at the kids, they dragged Lord Sparr quickly from the room.

The red wolves howled and chased them to the gates of the city. A moment later, the wolves trotted back.

Sparr was gone.

"Hooray!" the children of Droon cheered. They jumped for joy. "We did it! He's gone!"

Neal rushed over to them. "Slap me five, Droon kids!" he cried. They slapped Neal's hands. Then they did the same to one another.

Suddenly, the throne room went quiet.

Keeah looked up at Galen. She held the

empty velvet bag. "I have failed you again. My magic is gone. I am not worthy of being a wizard."

Everyone stared at the old man's icy face. Max covered his own.

Then the stony silence gave way to another sound.

The sound of wings.

Ten

Reverse the Curse!

The white falcon descended from the frosty air. She hovered above their heads.

"Keeah, my daughter!" the falcon said. "Zello, my king!"

Zello gazed up. "I have missed you!"

"Mother!" the princess said. "Sparr is gone, but his curse remains." She held up the empty velvet bag. "Galen is frozen. My people are frozen! The magic is all gone!"

"Keeah, my time here is almost done,"

the falcon said, fluttering up. "Already I have begun to change. I cannot help you now."

Eric, Julie, and Neal crowded around Keeah.

"How can I cure Galen?" she asked.

The falcon flapped her wings just above the princess. The bird's feathers started to shed. "Remember this always — *you are the magic*! Look into your heart, my child, and you will know."

The bird rose slowly up to the ceiling. Feathers fell away with every flap of her wings. They whirled around like snow-flakes in the cold air.

"When next you see me, I shall be in another form. Many trials lie ahead before I can undo this curse. Before I can be your mother again."

"You are my mother always!" Keeah said.

"Soon, I shall see you again!" her

mother called out. "Soon, Keeah! Soon, my brave king!"

A moment later, the falcon was no more than a sparkling blue light vanishing to nothing.

"Wow," Eric whispered.

The last white feather fluttered down slowly. Keeah reached up, clutched it, and held it tight.

Her father whispered to the air above them, "We will find you, my queen. We will help you."

Finally, Keeah looked at the old wizard. "A lightning bolt isn't going to help me now."

Max scuttled over to her. "Queen Relna said if you look into your heart you will know."

"I just thought of something else," said Neal. "I tasted the magic sugar after your mom zapped it. It was good, but pretty regular."

"Yes?" Keeah said.

"Well, I was thinking," Neal said. "What if the magic sugar was just, you know, sugar?"

"It worked when I unfroze the wolves," the princess said.

"But maybe for you, what you touch is magic," said Eric. "Because you are who you are."

Julie nodded. "It's like your mother said: '*You* are the magic.'"

Keeah blinked. "By myself? With no spells?"

"Yes!" the kids said together.

King Zello put his arm around his daughter. "I believe you can do it. I've watched you. You are your mother's daughter."

"Even Sparr said so," Neal added. "And he was scared of you."

Keeah took a deep breath. Then she bent down to the floor. She filled her hand with powdery flakes of snow. She stepped over to Galen and sprinkled the flakes over him.

The flakes danced slowly as they came down.

The ice began to melt from Galen's cheeks. His forehead. His eyes.

The old wizard's face softened. He smiled.

"Keeah!" he said. "I am alive again!"

"Master!" Max said, jumping up and down. "Welcome back to the world of the living!"

Keeah's eyes were wide with amazement. "If it works for you, then . . ." She rushed outside. The city around her lay frozen and white.

"My people! My city!" she called out.

Taking another handful of snow, she tossed it into the air. All at once, the whirling flakes became the soft white petals of apple blossoms!

The clouds swept away. Golden sunlight flooded the square.

Crrrack! Fountains suddenly crackled and spurted with fragrant water. Ice melted from the trees. Their bright green leaves swung loose. The air was full of sweet-scented flowers.

All the ice and snow across the city vanished under the warm sun.

"Spring is back in Jaffa City!" King Zello exclaimed. "Keeah, you have done it!"

Everyone who had been turned to ice began to move again. Soon there was laughter coming from every corner of the vast city.

"Awesome!" Eric said, smiling.

"Now, that's what I call true magic!" Neal said.

The kids shed their spider-silk coats and stood in the bright sunshine.

"This is more like it!" said Julie.

"And look!" Max pointed to the sky over the city's golden walls.

In the bright pink sky above a nearby hill were the rainbow-colored stairs.

The stairs to the Upper World.

The stairs back to Eric's house.

"I guess it's time," said Neal.

"We'd better go," Eric added, "so we can come back again as soon as possible!"

"Thank you for everything!" Galen said. "Once again, you have helped our world."

"And," boomed the king, "I proclaim that the next time you come to Jaffa City, it will be Eric and Julie and Neal Day!"

"It's a deal!" said Neal.

Everyone cheered. The crowd followed the three Upper Worlders to the foot of the magic stairway.

"Good-bye, for now," Keeah said, hugging her friends. "And come back soon!"

"That's a deal, too!" Eric said.

The three friends ran up the stairs. They entered the small room at the top.

Neal clicked the light switch. The room lit up.

Whoosh! The stairs vanished and the basement floor appeared beneath them.

The world of Droon was secret once more.

"What do you think Sparr's going to do with that amulet?" Neal asked when they slipped quietly out of the small room.

"I think we'll find out real soon," Julie said.

Sunlight streamed through the basement windows. The clock told them no time had passed.

Eric picked up the softball and tossed it. "Even though today was dangerous, I have to admit, it was pretty cool."

"Correction," said Neal, grabbing the ball and tossing it himself. "Cold, very cold."

"The word I would use is *icy*," Julie said. Then she stole the ball from Neal and ran up the stairs. "Last one in the backyard is a rotten egg!"

Eric and Neal shot looks at each other.

"Me first!" they both cried as they dashed up the stairs after her.

ABOUT THE AUTHOR

Tony Abbott is the author of more than two dozen funny novels for young readers, including the popular *Danger Guys* books and *The Weird Zone* series. Since childhood he has been drawn to stories that challenge the imagination, and, like Eric, Julie, and Neal, he often dreamed of finding doors that open to other worlds. Now that he is older — though not quite as old as Galen Longbeard — he believes he may have found some of those doors. They are called books. Tony Abbott was born in Ohio and now lives with his wife and two daughters in Connecticut.

THE SECRETS OF DROON

A New Series by Tony Abbott

$2.99 each!

Under the stairs, a magical world awaits you!

- ❏ BDK0-590-10839-5 #1: The Hidden Stairs and the Magic Carpet
- ❏ BDK0-590-10841-7 #2: Journey to the Volcano Palace
- ❏ BDK0-590-10840-9 #3: The Mysterious Island
- ❏ BDK0-590-10842-5 #4: City in the Clouds